CW01433492

WILD VALENTINE

WILD HEART MOUNTAIN: WILD RIDERS MC
BOOK SEVEN

SADIE KING

WILD VALENTINE

WILD RIDERS MC

She's the city girl looking for a story. He's the grumpy mountain man hurting from his past...

Only bad things happen on Valentine's Day, and this year looks to be no exception.

I've been sent to the middle of nowhere mountain to write a story on a reclusive ex-military artist who doesn't want to talk.

My job's on the line, I've got a pile of debt, and Mom needs me back in the city. But if I don't get Marcus to talk, I'm fired.

I've seen the way he looks at me, and I'm not above using my feminine curves to lure the mountain recluse out of his lair.

But once he's out, I might not want to put him back in.

As long as he doesn't find out what I'm really up to...

Wild Valentine is a grumpy/sunshine, city girl/mountain man, forced proximity instalove romance featuring a scarred ex-military hero and the innocent curvy girl he makes his Valentine.

Copyright © 2023 by Sadie King.

All rights reserved.

No part of this book may be reproduced in any form or by any electronic or mechanical means, including information storage and retrieval systems, without written permission from the author, except for the use of brief quotations in a book review.

Cover designed by Cormer Covers.

This is a work of fiction. Any resemblance to actual events, companies, locales or persons living or dead, are entirely coincidental.

Please respect the author's hard work and do the right thing.

www.authorsadieking.com

CONTENTS

1

HAZEL

"*O*nly a week till Valentine's Day."

Mom's bony fingers grasp mine so weakly, I barely feel the pressure. Panic rises in my chest at how feeble she is and I swallow it down, returning her weak smile as best I can.

"It's our lucky day, Hazel." Mom's voice is croaky and I lean forward to hear her better, hoping she doesn't see the distress in my face.

Valentine's Day is my mother's favorite day of the year. It's the day she met my father, it's the day they got married one year later, and it's the day I was born exactly one year after that.

But Valentine's Day is also the day my father was in a car accident three years ago that he never recovered from and the day my cat was run over two years ago. And it was Valentine's Day last year that

Mom was diagnosed with pancreatic cancer and given twelve months to live.

Valentine's Day has gone from being a happy day for my family to a curse.

But Mom refuses to acknowledge the bad stuff. She's at peace with her diagnosis and can't wait to be reunited with my father. She believes they're soul mates, and soul mates, "find each other no matter what realm they're in."

Yeah, my mom has gone all woo woo in the last few months, but it gives her comfort, so I hope like hell she's right.

I'm glad she has her newfound beliefs to comfort her, but I'm also terrified that in exactly one week, on Valentine's Day, Mom will choose to say goodbye to this 'realm,' as she calls it, to go join my father. Leaving me behind with the grief of being a grown up orphan.

But I can't let Mom see my pain. This could be her last week in this world, and I won't bring her down by being upset about it.

"Can I speak with you, Miss Lumley?"

The man in a suit isn't the doctor, and my heart sinks at the folded paper in his hand.

"Sure," I say brightly. "I'll be right back, Mom."

We duck into an office next to reception and I pull my shoulders back, trying to do the whole 'enti-

WILD VALENTINE

tled to be here, so what's your problem' thing that I'm never very good at.

"I'm sorry to bring this up at this difficult time, but your mother's bills are overdue."

I furrow my brow as if this is the first time I've heard about it, and I haven't been dreading this conversation for the last few days. Mom lost her insurance when she became too sick to work and lost her job. I've been covering the costs ever since.

"There must be something wrong with my account."

The man looks down and taps something into his computer. "It's the, ah, third payment that's been late…"

He leaves it hanging because I know what he's going to say next, and he at least has the decency to feel embarrassed about it.

"I can pay now if you have a machine."

I fumble in my wallet and pull out the credit card that I think has the most money on it.

"Because of your mother's continuing care and the, ah, late payments, we're going to have to ask for the next month in advance."

My heart sinks. I don't have that much money on credit, and I've got two cards maxed out already.

"And what if she…?"

I can't bring myself to say it. But the man looks at

3

me with a kind expression. "If you find you no longer need the bed, we will of course refund the money."

A sharp pain stabs my chest at the implication. Mom could be gone in a week, and it hits me like a freight train. My expression crumples, and no matter how hard I blink the tears fall.

The man looks horrified as he hands me a box of tissues.

"I'm so sorry, Miss Lumley, for this difficult time."

He looks like he really means it and I feel bad for the man, trying to do his job around so much grief.

"Just pay for the next two weeks, and we'll take it from there."

His kindness brings a fresh wave of tears, and he looks alarmed as I blow my nose a little too loudly into the tissues. I hand over the credit card, and despite the tears, hold my breath until it goes through.

My parents lived in the moment and didn't think much about the future. Since Dad passed, we've been living hand to mouth. The little money he did leave has been sucked up by Mom's treatment. At least I convinced her to see a proper doctor and managed to get her the full time care she needed.

The man taps at the computer, updating his file

and probably relieved he won't need to speak to me again for two weeks.

"I hear your mother is in good spirits, always making the staff laugh, so that's something."

It's amazing to me how Mom can keep up her good mood, which makes me dry my eyes. If she can face this with equanimity and laughter, then I can too.

"Thank you for your kindness."

As I stand up to leave his office, the wall calendar catches my eye. He's circled February 14th with a red marker in the shape of a heart.

Great. Everyone else looks forward to Valentine's Day, but my sense of dread returns as I leave the accountant's office.

I don't want Mom to see me with red eyes, and so I send her a quick text as I head outside. There's a missed call from Scott, my boss, and I call him back.

He's not as cool as he should be with the time I take off to spend with my dying mother, but he can't deny that my job is flexible. When you write for a magazine you can write on your own schedule, which is usually late at night for me. That's when inspiration hits.

"Hazel," he barks as soon as I pick up my phone. "Where the hell have you been?"

I had my phone turned off for like, twenty

minutes while I was visiting Mom on my lunch break, but Scott believes we should always be available.

"Sorry," I mumble. "Mom had a bad night and…"

"I've got an assignment for you. It could be big."

I swallow the annoyance at being cut off. I'm used to that from Scott by now. As the arts editor of *Culture Slam* magazine, art is his world. No matter how annoying he is, there's no denying that his focus and dedication has turned the magazine into New York's most prestigious arts magazine.

Despite my annoyance, my interest is piqued. I've been stuck on the small gallery scene since I started the job eighteen months ago, and I'm better than that. With an MA from Columbia, I'm itching to get into a proper story rather than covering yet another gallery opening. Also, there's an opening coming up. The senior arts journalist is leaving next month, and I want the position. I *need* the position. It comes with a substantial pay raise, and I'm counting on it to cover the credit card bills I've racked up paying for Mom's care.

"We were in this quaint little mountain town over the weekend." Scott's husband is a travel writer, and they're always going on mini breaks around the country.

"One side of the mountain is beautiful; the other

is a shit hole. No cell reception, the local industry is a sawmill, but tucked away on the mountain side is the most extraordinary restaurant and brewery..."

Scott has no problem talking when it's his life that's being talked about. I listen to him describe a craft brewery that's run by some motorcycle club and the art gallery they had out back. It sounds weird to me and dangerous. A bunch of hairy bikers into craft beer and art. It's probably a front for money laundering.

If that's the story he wants me to write, I'm not sure I'm up for it. It sounds dangerous and not in line with the magazine. I'm more into human interest stories than uncovering nefarious activities.

Scott gushes about the wood pieces they bought from a local artist, an ex-military guy who's gotten into wood carving.

"I want you to do a piece on the artist."

My breath hitches. It's the type of story I've been longing for. It's what I trained for. It's what I was born to do, uncovering the person behind the art, their inspiration and the reason why they create.

"I'll do it," I say without thinking.

"Good. I knew you'd be the woman for the job."

Pride makes my chest swell. Even though Scott's a dick, I still crave his praise. It would be stupid not to. He has the power to make or break my career.

"The artist is ex-military, so there's the angle. A bunch of veteran bikers making art on the side of a mountain."

My skin prickles at his words, and I know he's on to something. There's definitely a story here.

"Is the artist up for it?"

There's a pause. "Not exactly."

"What do you mean?"

"I've spoken to him, and he doesn't want to do the story. I thought, perhaps, sending a woman..."

He trails off, and my heart sinks. I'm not getting this opportunity because Scott thinks I'm ready. I'm getting the opportunity because I'm the only hetero-sexual woman on the team, and he thinks the fact that I've got boobs will make this red-blooded mountain man biker speak to me.

"When do you want me to go?"

Because no matter the reason, it's still a big break, and I hate myself for taking it.

"Tomorrow."

Wait. What?

"I can't go tomorrow. It's only a week till Valentine's Day." The day my mother potentially decides to leave this realm.

He scoffs. "We'll get you back for your big date. You've got three days."

I haven't told Scott how bad Mom is. He knows

8

she's sick, but it's a cutthroat industry. I'm lucky to have my job, and there are thousands of graduates, eager art fans just like me, who would snap his hand off for the opportunity.

But I can't go and leave Mom when she might only have a few days to live.

"I'm not sure..."

"A piece like this could get you recognized, Hazel. You pull this off, and I'll seriously consider you for the senior journalist role when it comes up."

My mind churns it over. Mom is getting excellent treatment; her last blood work was good, and everyone says she's got a great attitude. It's just me and the worry about this stupid Valentine's Day curse that has me thinking she might pass next week. And if she does fight it for longer, there are going to be more bills. I need all the money I can get.

If I go tomorrow, I can still be back with a few days to spend with Mom, just in case the worst happens.

"Just three days..."

"Yes," he snaps, getting cross now. "Unless you want me to ask Janey?"

Janey is the intern who's been working with us for a month. There no way she's getting this opportunity over me. If she's promoted over me, then I'm in the entry level pay position for God knows how long.

I'll never be able to keep paying for Mom's care. In the happy event that she lives longer, she'll end up in the overcrowded city hospice. And I refuse to let my mother end her life that way.

And if she passes, I'll have funeral expenses and even more credit card debt to pay off.

There's really only one answer I can give.

"I'll do it."

"Great," he says. "I'll email the details and have my assistant book your flight and accommodations."

"Okay, thanks..." But Scott's already hung up.

I head back in to tell Mom I'll be away for a few days, and a few moments later my phone pings.

Andreas has booked me on the 6am flight tomorrow to Charlotte, and then it's a train ride and a rental car from there. At least the Airbnb cabin he's booked looks cute.

May as well relax while you're there. he writes in the email. *I got you an early check in. If you need anything else, let me know.*

I bite my lower lip before asking him for an advance for expenses.

No problem. I won't tell boss man :)

At least Andreas has my back.

2

MARCUS

*T*he warbly notes of Celine Dion blast through the speaker behind the bar as Davis preps for the morning shift.

I usually don't mind that he has the radio turned up way too loud. The poor kid lost half his hearing, but why the fuck does every station have to play sappy love songs just because it's fucking Valentine's Day next week?

"Can you turn that shit off?"

Davis gives a wide grin. "What's the matter, Wood, not a fan of Celine?"

Not a fan of love more like it, but I'm not going to get into that with Davis. He's young. He'll learn in his own time that love is an illusion, and women can't be trusted.

Davis turns the volume down, thank God, just as

Calvin strides in, or Badge as we call him on the road.

His Sheriff's uniform is crumpled, and there's dark stubble on his usually smooth jaw.

"Double espresso," he says to Davis as he leans on the bar with his head in his hands.

"Trouble in town, Sheriff?"

Badge lets out a long sigh. "Just another bachelorette party."

Davis raises his eyebrows as he slides the steaming espresso cup toward Badge.

"Doesn't sound too bad, Sheriff."

Badge eyes the younger man warily. I'm sure to a twenty-something year old breaking up unruly bachelorette parties sounds like a wild time, but Badge is about the same age as me, thirty-four, and just as weary of women.

"They're wilder than the men some of them," he says. "And when you're responsible for the safety of those women on the mountain, it's no fun at all. Not when half of them are determined to get themselves into some kind of trouble."

"What was it this time?" I ask with mild amusement.

"They were getting rowdy by the lake. There were complaints from guests at The Lodge. They were so drunk on fruity cocktails not one of them would listen to me."

I chuckle despite myself, imagining Badge trying to tame a group of drunk women. He's a good looking guy and probably got propositioned by more than one.

"Had to get Axel to help me escort them back to their rooms. One of them was missing, and we spent the entire goddamn night looking for her. Turned out she'd fallen asleep in a patch of poison ivy. I've just come back from dropping her at the medical center in Hope. Goddamn bachelorette parties shouldn't be allowed."

I chuckle at my friend and MC brother, but he takes his job seriously. He really does feel responsible for those women.

"Is Prez in?" he asks.

I shake my head. We haven't seen much of the Prez since his honeymoon. Poor man's gotten all pussy whipped.

"I'm gonna take a shower upstairs and grab a few hours' sleep."

Badge heads off upstairs to the rooms above the bar. Anyone can use them as needed, and for Badge it means not having to trek home between shifts.

I pull out my phone and check the arrival time on

the Airbnb sight. Someone called Andreas is arriving in about an hour.

I've been renting out the small cabin on my land for the past few months. I don't need the income, but I like the company every now and again. I wonder what this Andreas is into. I like being there when my guests arrive so I can show them where to go for the good fishing spots, or hunting, or just walking if that's what they're here for.

The sound of heels clacking on tiles gets my attention.

My head jerks up as a vision of loveliness walks in from the back entrance door. She pauses in the doorway and glances about the place with a slight frown on her face.

"Are you guys open for coffee?"

Her voice is as sweet as her countenance. A black skirt clings to her curvy hips, and a ruffled pale green blouse showcases the rise of her large breasts.

She's short and curvy, but her heels give her an extra six inches. They're shiny like she just stepped off a sidewalk in a city instead of wandering into our mountain bar and MC headquarters.

"We don't open for another hour." I've never seen Davis move so fast, but he's over the side of the bar and practically salivating on the counter.

I give him a quick back off scowl.

"But I'm sure we can get you a coffee."

Her eyes dart to mine, and it's like an arrow hits my chest. I suck in my breath as the air rushes out of the room. She holds my gaze in a way that makes my entire body heat.

My heart thunders to a new beat, and one word rings clear in my head.

Mine.

"What would you like?"

Davis's voice breaks the spell, and the angel who just walked into our HQ glances over to him. The loss of her eyes on me feels like a cold wind hitting me in the face.

"Double latte with soy milk." She rattles off her order, and I detect a New York accent. My angel is far away from home, and I'm piqued with curiosity as to what the hell she's doing here. There's no car out front.

"How'd you get here?"

Her gaze shifts back to mine, and I notice the dark shadows under them. There's a little frown creasing her forehead that I long to run my thumb over and smooth out.

"The back door was open," she explains. "My rental car's out back."

She must have driven in the back entrance while I was talking to Badge.

"I thought you'd be open. It's..." She checks her phone. "After ten."

I chuckle at her confusion. She must be used to getting anything she likes 24-7

"This isn't New York."

Her frown deepens. "How do you know where I'm from?"

My gaze travels lazily up her body from the polished heels to the silk stockings, the tight skirt that restricts movement too much to be any use on a mountain, the carefully ironed blouse with the pretty but useless ruffles on the sleeves and the over-sized purse that's not a backpack, which is what most people carry on the mountain.

"Just a lucky guess."

She smiles then, and my breath hitches. My New York angel is even more lovely when she smiles. Her blue eyes light up, and the dark smudges under them seem to fade away.

"Am I over-dressed for the mountain?" she teases.

"Just a little."

Davis hands her a coffee, and she closes her eyes to inhale the scent. As she takes a deep breath she stretches her neck, exposing a pale throat that makes my pulse race. I long to run my tongue up the line of her neck to that sensitive bit behind the ear.

Christ. What's this woman doing to me? I've

known her less than five minutes, and I'm already fantasizing about kissing her throat and ripping that ridiculous skirt off her. I've kept away from women for the last twelve years, and for good reason, but one look at this beauty and all reason goes out the window.

"What brings you to Wild Heart Mountain?"

Her eyes flutter open, and she purses her lips together to blow on the hot coffee.

My cock hardens at the sight of her plump lips, thinking about all the things I'd like her to do with her mouth.

"I'm here for work."

I've got no idea what kind of work could bring a New York angel to this side of the mountain. I'm about to ask when she takes a sip of her coffee and moans.

She fucking moans, a soft little sound that has my cock twitching in my suddenly too tight jeans.

"That's good coffee."

I slide off the stool, because it's too uncomfortable to keep sitting.

Her eyes follow me as I stand up and widen as she takes in my full height. Yup, I'm a big bastard, and next to me my angel seems tiny. She's all short and curvy, and even with the killer heels, I tower above her.

She swallows, and her gaze darts away. It comes to rest on the vintage bike on the wall. She walks over to it and I follow with my eyes, enjoying the way her skirt hugs her ass.

She takes in her surroundings, scrutinizing the pictures on the wall and peering at the inscriptions.

"This is the Wild Riders Motorcycle Club Headquarters."

She states it as fact and I raise my eyebrows, wondering how a girl from New York has heard about our MC.

She leans forward, staring at one of the photos. It's from a Veteran's Day ride and we're straddling our bikes, kitted out in our military gear rather than our MC jackets, ready to hit the road.

"Veterans," she says softly, like she's talking to herself.

"That's right."

She jumps at the sound of my voice, not aware that I had come up behind her. She spins around, and I'm so close that her breasts brush my chest. She lets out a gasp of surprise but doesn't step back.

"Sorry I scared you."

Her eyes are more startling up close. One's deeper blue than the other, but there's no denying the dark smudges underneath. My angel has troubles, and I can't wait to soothe them.

"Why are you here...?"

I don't even know her name. The woman takes a ragged breath, and her lips part. My eyes dart to them, so plump and sweet and agonizingly close.

"Is the coffee alright? I didn't know if you wanted it milkier," Davis calls from the bar. I grit my teeth; the boy's timing is incredibly poor. The spell is broken, and the woman steps back.

"No. Thank you. It's perfect as it is."

She darts back to the bar and retrieves her coffee from the counter. She takes a long sip, determinedly looking forward.

"What's your name?"

I follow her to the bar and lean my elbows against it. Trying to be casual while this woman has me all twisted up inside.

It's been a long time since a woman had me in a spin, and that didn't end well. But I ignore the warning from my brain as my body takes over, making me tongue-tied and hot and hard all at once.

"Hazel," she says.

"Hazel." It's a beautiful name. It suits my angel. "Why are you here, Hazel?"

She sips her coffee and places the mug down slowly.

"I'm looking for someone. Marcus Wild. I heard he's a member of the MC."

My name on her lips makes my chest expand and my cock lengthen. My angel is here for me. How could I be so lucky?

Then it all slides together.

"You're from the magazine."

I push away from the bar as my chest deflates. My angel is here for me, but only to interview me for some goddamn vanity magazine. To exploit my story to sell copies of their pretentious magazine.

She nods. "I'm Hazel Lumley, arts journalist for *Culture Slam* magazine."

She holds out a hand, and I stare at it until she draws it back in. The frown reappears on her face, but this time I'm not so eager to wipe it off.

"I told your boss I'm not interested, so stop harassing me."

Her eyes go wide, and I almost feel sorry for her. "I'm not harassing you…"

Tracking me to the MC headquarters sure feels like harassment to me. "You're kidding, right?"

"Just give me five minutes of your time…"

"Five minutes won't change anything." I hate to do this to her, and I really hope she doesn't lose her job. But there's no way I'm talking to that magazine. "I'm sorry you've wasted your time, Hazel, but it's a no."

I grab my jacket off the back of the stool and

pocket my phone. My guest is turning up soon, and I want to be there to greet him.

A pang of regret tugs at me as I stride past my New York angel. But that's women for you. Duplicitous.

It's best she gets back on the plane and straight home to New York where she belongs.

3

HAZEL

"*Well*, that went well," I mutter to myself as the incredibly hot biker who turns out to be the moody artist storms out of the bar.

I watch his retreating ass, finding some comfort in his succulent looking butt cheeks pressed against his tight jeans as he stalks out the door. At least I got to watch his ass, even if I didn't get the story.

"You want anything else?" the sweet but oblivious man behind the counter asks. "The kitchen will be opening in half an hour."

"This is fine. Thank you for making it for me."

Any self-respecting cafe in New York would have been open since five to get the early morning customers, but I guess things don't work that way in the mountains.

I came straight to the MC headquarters in the hopes of catching Marcus, but I didn't expect him to be so against the idea of speaking to me. Scott made it sound like all he needed was a bit of female persuasion. He didn't tell me he flat out doesn't want to talk.

I nibble on my fingernail, and I contemplate my next move. It's clear Marcus feels harassed, thanks to Scott, no doubt. If I give him some space and a bit of time to think about it, he might come around.

He probably feels hijacked by me turning up at his club's HQ. People don't like being taken by surprise. Now that he knows I'm here, he might come around to the idea of talking. In the meantime, I can find out a little about the man.

"Is he always that moody?" I ask the guy behind the bar. He seems not to hear me as he pulls a tray of glasses out of the dishwasher. That's when I notice the hearing aids on both his ears.

All the MC members are veterans, Scott said, and I wonder if this man is too. He doesn't seem much older than me, in his early or mid-twenties, and I wonder if he lost his hearing in the war.

My curiosity's buzzing with questions, and I get a tingle down my spine that lets me know I'm onto a good story. Scott was right. Veterans in a motorcycle club is good human interest angle.

I wait for the young man to turn around and try again.

"Are you a member of the MC too?" It's obvious he is by the leather jacket he's wearing with the Wild Rider's emblem, but it's a conversation starter.

He breaks into a smile and slaps the patch on the left breast of his jacket. "Yes ma'am."

I've never been addressed as ma'am in my life. I like it. No one's this polite in New York.

"Were you in the military?" I ask cautiously. I'm not sure how much he'll want to talk, but the man only nods and taps his left hearing aid.

"Have the hearing loss to prove it."

There's a sudden noise from behind the bar, half yawn half snarl.

The man laughs at my startled expression as a giant dog lifts itself off the floor and stretches. "Don't mind Hercules. He's just woken up, haven't you boy."

He scratches the dog behind the ears and it rearranges itself, settling back down by the man's feet.

We fall into an easy conversation. I ask the boy about the club and he talks eagerly, telling me it's like one big family, how it gave him a new focus and purpose when he got released from the military. He was a prospect for eighteen months, doing menial tasks and proving himself until he was voted in.

I downloaded some articles and did my research on the plane, reading up about MC clubs and the hierarchy within them and the activities they get up to--usually running guns or drugs. But this one seems different.

It's feels less threatening than I thought it would, and they run a restaurant and brewery. It's hardly dangerous stuff.

We talk for about twenty minutes before Davis, as I found out he's called, has to get things ready for opening. I thank him for his time and head out the back to my rental car.

The smell of hops hangs in the air in the court-yard from the brewery that's out back. There's also a mechanic's shop and in the far corner an art studio. It must be where Scott picked up Marcus's pieces, and I head there now.

The art gallery is tucked into a corner of the compound. There are shelves of watercolors and local crafts as well as cute vintage drawings and memorabilia. One entire shelf is woodwork with larger pieces sitting on the floor.

There are all sorts of animals, an owl in flight and a bear on its haunches, but it's the carved warriors that make me gasp in surprise.

They're exquisite and lifelike, their face etched in hard lines, grim looks, and one in agony. I can see why Scott got excited, especially considering the story behind the artist: a military veteran carving effigies of his experiences at war. Showing the grim side of the American war machine.

My spine tingles but not just with the excitement of the story.

Marcus carved these. The gruff looking biker who towered over me with a thick beard and muscular arms. He looks like he'd crush a piece of wood rather than sculpt delicate art out of it.

I long to know what's going on behind the exterior of the hard mountain man. And it's not just for professional reasons that I'm curious. The man made me *feel* things. Deep, dark, delicious things that stirred my stomach and tugged at my core. Things I haven't felt for a man before.

"Can I help you?"

I look up and blink in surprise. The woman in front of me is like something straight out of the pages of a 1950s magazine. Her polka-dot dress flares at the waist, and her hair's half pinned back in rolls. She bounces a toddler on her hip who's got the same dark curls as her mamma.

"What can you tell me about the artist?"

"Marcus Wild." The toddler whines, and she sets

her down on the floor. The little girl crawls over to a play area in the corner.

"He's a local guy. His family owns the sawmill, and he's one of the MC. He lives by himself in a cabin in the woods."

I swallow, trying to keep my voice steady, but it goes up an octave. "By himself? He's not married?"

She shakes her head and smiles, her eyes dancing as if she can read my thoughts. "No. No girlfriend either."

My cheeks redden, and I set the piece down quickly. I'm an open book when it comes to the mountain man I just met.

"Thank you."

I retreat out of the shop. I'll come back another time for more information once I can control my blushing cheeks.

Besides, I was up at 4am to catch my flight, and I'd love a hot shower and a nap.

The woman gives me a knowing smile as she watches me go.

"Come see us again," she calls after me.

Ten minutes later, my hybrid Kia rental turns onto the road that the GPS has given me for the Airbnb. Andreas warned me it was remote, but this is positively in the middle of nowhere. I haven't passed another dwelling for the last five minutes, and the driveway snakes around further into the woods.

At least the GPS is still working.

The driveway is narrow and I take it slow. If anyone was coming the other way, I'd be toast. Suddenly the towering trees open up, and I slow down as a cabin comes into view.

It looks like something from a postcard. Wooden slats perfectly joined with the second story roof, which is slanted in perfect eaves. A porch runs around the edge, and comfortable looking outdoor furniture gives it a homely look. I wonder who lives there and what kind of life it would be to have place like this as your permanent home.

But it's not the main cabin I'm staying in.

To the left is a short drive that leads to a smaller cabin, and this is what I pull up in front of. It's just as cute, a smaller version of the main house.

I cut the engine and lean over the steering wheel to admire my home for the next three days. At least if I can't get Marcus to talk, I'll still get a relaxing break.

I get out of the car, shivering in the cool mountain air. My heels catch on pine needles, and one spike picks up a leaf. I carry it for a few steps before pulling it off. That never happens in New York.

I'm staring at the instructions on my phone from Andreas when there's a familiar voice behind me.

"Who gave you my address?"

I give a squeak of surprise, and my phone drops to the ground. I spin around to find Marcus; his jacket is open, his shirt clinging relentlessly to his muscular chest. There's a layer of perspiration that shows the outlines of his nipples. He must have been chopping wood or some other extremely masculine, mountain man type activity. My pulse races and my thighs clench together to contain the pull I feel down there.

My mouth drops open and closed like a fish's before I drag my eyes up to his face.

His eyebrows are knit together, and his eyes flash dangerously.

"I'm staying here," I manage to get out as I bend down to retrieve my phone.

The screen is cracked, which is the last thing I need. I hope like hell it still works, because I can't afford to replace my phone anytime soon.

His brows furrow in confusion. "Then who the fuck is Andreas?"

My stomach drops to the floor. He thinks I'm stalking him, and this isn't going to be good for my story. So much for giving him space.

"Andreas is my assistant. Well, technically Scott's, but…"

His eyes narrow at the mention of Scott. "He found out I have an Airbnb. That son of a bitch."

I've heard Scott called worse, but in this case, I don't think it was intentional.

"No. Andreas booked this; Scott had nothing to do with it."

He rubs his beard and looks like he doesn't believe me. "This is harassment."

I hold my hands up, suddenly panicked. If I come back with no story, that's one thing, but no story and a lawsuit? I can't let that happen.

"I didn't know this was your place, I swear. Andreas booked it for me. He thought the cabin looked cute. Like a hallmark movie."

I'm babbling, but it seems to work, Marcus keeps his eyebrows pushed together, but it's more of a curious, what the heck is this babbling woman doing on my property look than anger.

"I'm really sorry. I know how it looks, but I won't harass you anymore. I'll go straight back to New York if that's what you want. But I'm cold and sweaty all at once, and I've been up since four, and I'd really just love a hot shower before I go."

He shakes his head slowly, and the anger's gone out of him.

"Your boss is an asshole."

"Yup." I nod in agreement. Marcus isn't the first person to say those words to me.

"I won't do your story, so stop asking. But I won't kick you out either. If you want to stay, you can. It looks like you need a vacation."

He squints at me and I turn away, embarrassed. Is it that obvious that I've barely been sleeping? That the worry over Mom and the stress about the bills has me biting my nails down and tossing and turning all night.

"Thank you," I say.

He hands me a key, and our fingers touch briefly. A spark leaps from his hand onto mine, and I pull back at the shock of it. My gaze darts to his, and he's looking at me with a new intensity.

He felt it too.

Whatever *it* was.

Did I just experience some kind of animal attraction? My curious mind goes into overdrive, and I long to touch him again to see if it happens again.

"WiFi password's on the fridge. One of the rooms is made up, and there are spare towels in the bathroom."

I don't get the opportunity to test my hypothesis about the spark because Marcus turns and strides to the main cabin, taking the last of my hopes with him.

So much for using my feminine wiles to get him to talk. This story is dead in the water.

After dumping my luggage, I give Mom a call. She's doing well, she tells me, and feeling stronger. She even went out for a walk earlier. I'm pleased to hear that. It makes me feel better about being away from her for a few days.

She wants to know all about the mountain and the artist, and I don't have the heart to tell her it's not going well.

Instead, I tell her about the MC clubhouse and the cute cabin, leaving out the bit about the grumpy owner.

After we walk, I make the call I've been dreading.

Scott picks up on the first ring.

"Tell me good news, Hazel."

I bite my lower lip.

"He's not gonna talk, Scott. It's a flat out no. I may as well fly back tonight."

There's silence on the other end of the line, and I hold my breath.

"Not acceptable."

I hang my head. I hate letting him down, but I don't see how I'm going to get the story without Marcus.

"I've spoken to some of the other club members. It's amazing what they've got going on here. There's a young man..."

"Is he an artist?"

Scott's words are clipped.

"No."

"Then I'm not interested. Get Marcus to speak. It's his story I want. The veteran artist whose tortured soul comes out in his work. It's going front page for Memorial Day weekend. It'll make him famous; he'll sell a ton of pieces and makes loads of money. Have you told him that?"

"I don't think he wants..."

"People always want something," Scott says in what's supposed to be a wise tone.

"I don't think he's going to change his mind, Scott."

"You better hope he does, Hazel. You want to be writing up gallery reviews forever? Because that's what you'll be doing if you don't get this story. And if I've wasted three day's worth of expenses flying you there, it's grounds for firing."

His words hit me like a blow to the chest. I thought I might risk not getting a promotion, but losing my job...

"You can't do that." But I'm not sure that's true. If

Culture Slam wants to get rid of someone, they'll find a way.

"I need journalists who can get me a story, Hazel. You're no good on my team if you can't do that."

The thought of Mom's bills swims in my head. The credit card debt, the medication, the pain she'll be in if I can't afford her meds.

"But how do I get him to talk if he doesn't want to?" It comes out as a whisper, my throat constricted by the possibility of losing my job.

I can practically hear Scott smirk down the phone. "You're a smart woman, Hazel. I'm sure you'll think of something."

He hangs up, leaving me heavy with dread. I have to get this story. Mom's depending on me. I have to get Marcus to talk.

4

MARCUS

a knock at the door makes me look up from my laptop. I close the browser with *Culture Slam's* webpage on it, not wanting whoever it is to see that I've been reading every piece by Hazel Lumley.

She's a good writer, but she's only done gallery openings and a few interviews with collectors. I wonder why she was sent to get my story.

I pull open the door and stop dead in my tracks at the sight before me. Hazel's wrapped in one of the fluffy bath towels from the rental cabin. The moss green towel barely covers her full figure. The pale skin on her bare shoulders is dimpling in the cool air.

My gaze sweeps down her body taking in the line

of the towel that pushes up her cleavage and the way she's clasping it across her body as if the thing might fall off at any minute. The towel's too short and her thick thighs are on display, as luscious as I knew they would be when I first saw her in that tight skirt.

My mouth goes dry, and I'm instantly hard. I want to pull her inside and out of the cold, and at the same time I want to rip the towel off her to discover if she's wearing panties underneath.

"There's no hot water."

My gaze lifts to her face and the innocent wide eyes.

She has no idea what she's doing to me, knocking on my door in nothing but a towel. If I thought she was even remotely interested, I'd rip it off her and take her here on the doorstep.

I swallow hard, not even attempting to keep my eyes off the soft rise of her breasts that swell, tantalizingly soft and creamy, above the towel.

She's saying something but I must have missed it, because she's looking at me expectantly.

"Huh?"

I draw my gaze back to her face, and she's staring at me with a slight smile.

"I said there's no hot water."

Hot water, right. My mind's foggy, and all I can

think about is yanking the towel off her and finding out what those breasts feel like cupped in my hands.

"I went to take a shower…"

She speaks slowly, like she's talking to a child, and finally I realize what she's saying and why she's here.

"There's no hot water?"

She looks nervous, and I guess she should with the way I'm ogling her. With a monumental effort, I keep my gaze on her face. She gives me a half smile, but her eyes flicker to the side.

She's nervous.

She should be, showing up on a stranger's doorstep in nothing but a towel. I'm twice her size. I could pull it off and push her against the door…

"Do you think you can fix it?"

"Huh?"

"Fix the shower."

She puts a hand on her hip in exasperation and the towel slips a little, opening at the seam and giving me a flash of upper thigh. I make out a dark spot between her legs, a glimpse of wiry dark hair.

No panties.

"Fuck." I turn away and run a hand through my hair.

This woman.

If I don't get her out of here, I'm going to slam her up against the wall and take her right in the doorway.

"I'll grab my tool kit. Meet you over there."

"Thank you," she calls after me as I retrieve my tool kit from under the sink. When I come back, she's still standing in the doorway.

"For god's sake, put some clothes on."

Her eyes bug out of her head, but there's a small smile on her lips. I wonder if she came over here on purpose to seduce me.

I'd be so lucky. I'm just trying to give myself an excuse to take her up against the wall.

No, she's too innocent for that. Hazel went to take a shower, and the water was cold. She's not trying to seduce an old grouchy mountain man like me.

I stride toward her cabin, and I hear her bare feet crunching on the leaves behind me. She'll catch her death out here walking around in the cold in nothing but a flimsy towel.

When we get to her cabin, I don't dare to look back. I toe my boots off and head into the bathroom. I had it fitted out a few months back when I started renting the place out.

The property came with both cabins and a shed,

which I've turned into a workshop. I don't need the money. I have shares in the family sawmill, and with my army pension and my carvings, I have everything I need. But it can get lonely on the mountain, and I like the company of an occasional visitor.

But right now I'm regretting my life choices.

The sexiest woman I've ever met is behind me in nothing but a towel. My knuckles turn white from gripping my toolbox so hard to keep from gripping her.

I head to the bathroom and try the shower. The knob is turned all the way to cold, so I switch it to hot and turn the shower on, staring at the water and waiting to see if it'll heat up.

She's behind me. I can tell by the scent of coffee and rose water. But I don't dare look at her. Not if I want to avoid a lawsuit.

After a few minutes, steam rises off the water. I put my hand under the shower, and it's scalding.

I risk a look at Hazel and she's still in the goddamn towel, leaning casually against the bathroom door.

"You've got to turn it to the left for hot."

"Oh." She looks sheepish, biting her lower lip.

I frown. She's a smart girl. I can tell by the way she writes. How'd she get the tap wrong? Maybe it's the other way around where she comes from. All I know is I have to get out of here before I do something stupid.

"I'll leave you alone to have your shower."

"Stay." Her voice comes out as a whisper that makes my cock jerk.

Her eyes widen, and her hand flies to her mouth. "I mean, stay and have a coffee with me. I'll only be a minute. I'd like to explain."

If I stay here with only a wall between us knowing she's naked in that shower, there's no telling what I might do.

"I can't."

Her brow furrows in that little frown she does when she's not getting her way. With the dark smudges under her eyes, she suddenly looks tired. Maybe I'm being too harsh. It can't be easy coming all this way only to be turned down.

"Look, Hazel, I'm not going to do the interview. Not even for a pretty girl in a towel."

She looks down, and I can't read her expression. I wonder if she came over in the towel on purpose to get my attention. It's something a woman would do.

"I'm sorry you've come all this way." Or am I? My head's been in a spin ever since she walked into HQ this morning. I'm not going to give her the interview, but I'd sure as hell like to spend some time with her. "I'm not going to talk to you about my work, but since you're here, let me show you the mountain."

Her chin lifts up, but she looks defeated, resigned to some fate that I can only guess at. If she loses her job because of this, then her boss is more of an asshole than I thought.

But that doesn't explain the worry in her eyes and the dark smudges. She looks like she needs some fun. Whatever's got her up at night, she needs to put it out of her mind for a while.

"Then your trip won't be wasted."

Steam's filling up the bathroom now, heating me up and doing nothing to help the fact that I'm on fire just being around her.

"I've never been to the mountains."

The confession floors me. But I shouldn't be surprised. She's from New York. There's so much to show her here.

"Good. I'll collect you after breakfast tomorrow."

She smiles, and a look of triumph crosses her face.

"I'm not changing my mind about the interview," I warn before she gets any ideas. "But I will show you my mountain."

I leave her to the shower and walk uncomfortably back to my cabin, trying not to let it show that I've got a massive boner.

As soon as I'm inside, I take my aching cock from my jeans and think about Hazel soaping herself down in the shower as I tug at myself.

My release comes fast, but it's not satisfying. It won't be until I've had the real thing.

5

HAZEL

*T*error clenches my stomach and rises up my chest, tumbling out of my throat in a strangled scream.

Trees fly past below me, my feet almost skimming their branches. As I whiz over the canopy clutching the thick rope, the terror turns to exhilaration and the scream to a long whoop. Then I giggle, and by the time I reach Marcus, grinning on the platform and ready to catch me, I'm laughing so hard my belly aches.

My feet find purchase on the platform, and Marcus's strong arms wrap around me as I come to the end of the zip line.

"That was insane!"

I'm laughing so hard, and I'm not sure why. I

guess it's the adrenaline coursing through my veins because I just jumped off a perfectly good wooden platform and flew over the trees.

"Let's go again."

Marcus laughs at my eagerness, but I'm being serious.

For one joyful moment, I forgot why I was here. I forgot the story I'm supposed to be writing, I forgot my mother dying in a hospital bed, and I forgot the massive bills pilling up and waiting for me in New York. For one joyful moment, it was just me flying through the trees on a zip line.

"All right, my little adrenaline junkie." Marcus grins at me so hard it makes my heart squeeze. "We've got to get around the rest of the course, but if you want, at the end, we can go around again."

"Yes please," I say without hesitation.

I've never done anything like this in my life. There's no zip-lining over a forest in New York. But it's not just the zip-lining that's got me pumped. The more time I spend with Marcus, the more I fall for the surly mountain man.

We're high above the trees on wooden platforms, just me, Marcus, and the instructor. We're in harnesses and attached to the safety ropes in two places.

There's not a lot of room on these wooden platforms, and as I move to the next line, my boobs brush up against Marcus.

My entire body shudders at the contact. Even through the layers of clothing, my body's on fire. I'm not sure if the adrenaline comes from zip-lining through the trees or being this close to Marcus.

"Remind me to buy you a sky dive for your birthday."

My stomach drops at the reminder of my birthday. It's in five days, the same day as Valentine's Day. Marcus senses the change in my mood.

"What did I say?"

I'm not ready to tell him about my mother and the Valentine's Day curse, not yet. "My birthday's next week."

He chuckles until he sees my expression. "You don't like birthdays?"

"Not ones on Valentine's Day."

Marcus looks pained for a moment. The instructor comes up to secure me to the next rope and blocks my view of him.

When I see him again, he's smiling.

"You want to go first on this one?"

He doesn't pry about Valentine's Day, which is a relief.

The next challenge is a walk over the forest on nothing but a thin metal wire with ropes to hold onto on either side.

If you'd told me I'd be doing this yesterday morning as I navigated the early New York traffic to LaGuardia airport, I'd never have believed you.

When Marcus brought me here, a million excuses went through my head. I'm too heavy. I'm scared of heights. I'm not adventurous. He ignored all my protests, because it turns out none of them are true. If it can take Marcus's weight, it can take mine, and I'm not actually scared of heights. I've just never had the opportunity to be on anything high apart from an office building with thick windows.

As I shimmy across the thin rope, I wonder how I'm going to explain the Valentine's Day curse to Marcus. There's a curse on my family, and we were good for a while, but now only bad things happen on Valentine's Day? I'm going to sound crazy.

We get to the next platform, and I slide in beside the instructor as Marcus expertly maneuvers across. He slides across the rope not once looking down, sure-footed and confident. He's agile for a big man, and I guess that's his army training.

"What did you do in the military?"

He doesn't answer, and when I look up, he's eyeing me warily.

"Nice try, angel."

I'm not sure when he started calling me angel or why, but it makes my tummy go all fluttery and my cheeks heat.

"I wasn't..."

I'm about to say I wasn't prying for information, but I'm not sure that's true. Isn't that exactly what I'm doing?

I went to his cabin wrapped in a towel for the express purpose of getting him to ask me out. I'm not stupid. I saw the way he looked at me in the bar. I hate to say it, but Scott was right. Marcus is a hot-blooded man, and if anything's going to get the story it's my feminine wiles, or at least my boobs.

I feel a twinge of uneasiness at the thought. It's not really ethical to turn up in a towel to get his attention. I was half hoping it wouldn't work, that he wouldn't be just another hot-blooded male. I was both elated and disappointed when he asked me out today.

But it's not just because I need this story. *I like him.* How could I not? He's hot and muscular and artistic. He's a deep thinker with a past. He's thoughtful and kind, and did I mention his muscles? His arms look like they could break me in half while his hands could mold me...

"Sorry." I shake the thought of his hands on me out of my head. "I'm naturally curious."

He harrumphs at me, and I wonder if he's going to open up. God knows I need this story and this promotion, but I'm uneasy about it. I hate myself for tricking him into spending time with me. Even if I am enjoying myself.

"The next one is the longest zip line on the course," the instructor says as he latches my harness to the wire.

Marcus steps onto the platform, and his presence looms over me. We're so close but there's nowhere to go, nowhere to back up to even if I wanted to.

"Of course you are," he murmurs.

His thumb brushes at my cheek, tucking away a strand of hair away that's come lose from my helmet.

"I'm not doing the story, Hazel, but if you're curious, come by for dinner and I'll show you my work. Off the record."

My heart's thumping in my chest so loud I think the whole forest must hear it.

He wants to talk. He wants to share his story, but he doesn't want me to write about it. I should push for more. Scott would want me to. Play hard to get and insist I won't spend time with him unless he agrees to do the feature. But as I look into his troubled eyes, I can't do it.

I'm not cutthroat like Scott needs me to be. I want the story, but I won't breach this man's trust. Maybe I'm not cut out to be a feature writer after all. I'm not ruthless enough.

"What's wrong?"

Marcus frowns and I look down, embarrassed that my every thought is written across my face.

"Nothing," I mumble.

If it was just the job, it would be a no brainer. But then I think about mom, her sunken expression, spending her last days in a rundown facility. Why does life have to be so complicated?

"Dinner sounds good." I lift my eyes to his and force a smile.

"Off the record," he reiterates.

"Off the record," I repeat and hope like hell I can keep my promise.

There's a cough behind me, and I turn to find the instructor staring at us pointedly.

I give a giggle like we've been caught.

"Who's going first?" he asks.

"Me!"

I step forward and allow him to attach me to the next zip line. For today, I'm going to enjoy myself. I'm doing something fun with a hot, interesting man.

For one day, I can just be Hazel Lumley, a

twenty-five-year-old, kind of chubby city girl enjoying a few days in the mountains.

But as I fly over the canopy, I can't shake the uneasy feeling in the pit of my stomach, my conscience nibbling at me, telling me what I'm doing is wrong.

6
HAZEL

*T*he aroma of thyme and rosemary hangs in the air and heat from the fire warms my cheeks, making them glow hot, but it's the presence of Marcus next to me that makes my skin burn.

We cooked dinner together in his cabin, a chicken stew which he garnished with herbs from his own garden. It turns out he's an excellent cook, which doesn't surprise me. The man's creative and good with his hands. My body shivers when I think about what those big, creative hands would feel like on my body.

His cabin is sparse but tastefully furnished. A coffee table carved from a single hunk of wood sits by the blazing fire. We eat cross-legged on the rug, needing to be close to the fire to warm us up.

There's no hint of a woman here, and I'm dying

to ask him about his status. The woman at the studio told me he was unmarried, but I want to be sure. But it's hard to casually ask if he has a girlfriend without being completely obvious about why I want to know.

Because I like him.

"So, you're telling me that your family is cursed and something bad is going to happen on Valentine's Day, but it wasn't always a bad curse because it's also your birthday?"

I hide my face in my hands. It sounds even more ridicules said out loud by a practical mountain man. But he pushed me about my birthday, and so I told him everything except for the bit about Mom and the bills.

"Something like that."

I peek at him though my fingers, waiting for the laughter, but Marcus nods solemnly. "Sounds reasonable."

He's teasing me, and I grab the cushion behind my back and swipe him with it.

"You know it's only a day, right? And it has no power if you don't give it any."

I tilt my head, thinking about his words. They make sense. They make so much sense. But telling my heart that, or my mother, just doesn't work.

Thinking of Mom makes my chest hurt, so I change the subject.

"How about you? Why do you hate Valentine's Day?"

He raises his eyebrows in surprise. "How do you know I hate Valentine's Day?"

"Got ya!"

He throws the cushion back at me, and I dodge it laughing. "It was a guess. Your nose does this little wrinkle every time I mention it."

He looks half impressed and half indignant. "Does not."

"Valentine's Day." He has a momentary look of disgust on his face. "See!"

His eyes go wide, bewildered. "Son of a... am I that transparent?"

"No. I'm ultra-observant. Part of what makes me good at my job."

I'm proud of my ability to read people. I have a high degree of empathy, and that makes me both excellent at telling a human interest story and terrible at actually getting the story, it turns out.

He shakes his head, looking at me with new respect, which makes me feel all kinds of warm inside. I want to impress this man; I want to so badly.

"You could read palms with that skill."

He's avoided the question. He hasn't told me why he hates Valentine's Day, but I'm not going to push. It's one more mystery in the line of mysteries about Marcus Wild.

It's cozy here on the couch. We've talked all night, avoiding the topics of his military life, his artwork, and my mother expertly. It's like a dance we're doing around each other.

But it's a dance I like. I wish this moment could be frozen forever and kept in a snow globe in my memory. Just two people sitting on a couch, talking and laughing.

But I have a job to do, and I need to keep pushing.

"You promised you'd show me your artwork."

He nods. "I did. Come on."

We shrug on our coats, and I follow him into the darkness to the workshop behind his cabin.

The workshop smells like wood resin and beeswax with a hint of oil, like a condensed forest, earthy and comforting. Which is exactly how Marcus smells when you get as close to him as I did on the zip-lining platform.

He flicks on the lights and the space comes into sharp focus, making me catch my breath.

The walls are lined with large chunks of wood, stored and ready for carving. There's a long work bench and carvings in various states sitting among piles of sawdust. His tools are left out on the bench, ready to be picked up at a moment's notice.

On the left are finished pieces waiting to be varnished. There are a variety of lifelike animals, including a slinking fox with its ears back, the muscles of its legs so realistic I expect it to move at any moment. An owl in flight stares at me with wide eyes.

But it's the people that capture my attention, the carved torsos, upper bodies, and faces of men in military uniforms. The one currently on the work bench has an arm swinging in motion, clasping a rifle as the head turns, the face an expression of grim resignation at whatever it sees approaching.

In another one, a man covers his face with his hands. The eye peering between his fingers is wide with horror.

They're beautiful and devastating all at once. My spine tingles and for a moment I'm transported to the dessert, to whatever modern battlefield these depict. I can almost smell the fear, taste the blood, and hear the screams.

"Marcus..." My eyes turn to him, and there are tears in them. "Are these...?"

I don't even need to ask. He nods. "Yup." His

voice is clipped, holding the pain inside. "All from memory."

My hands go to my mouth as I begin to understand the horror he must have seen. We hear so little about modern warfare. It's in far off countries, and we barely see the consequences. But these bring it all to life, the reality of being at war, of sending our soldiers to fight.

"How long were you in the military?"

I hold my breath, not sure if he'll answer. But it's not because of the story that I ask. It's because he's baring his soul with these effigies and I want to heal him, to soothe him, to take away some of his pain.

"Twelve years." He turns away from the table of warriors. "Too long."

And the rigidness of his back tells me everything I need to know. He lost friends over there. He saw death, and it wasn't pretty or noble. It was a beast that clawed into his soul and haunts him still.

Tentatively, I put a hand on his shoulder. "I'm sorry."

He turns to face me, and his face is in shadow. "I don't like to talk about it, Hazel."

He's breathing hard, and I hear all that's unsaid.

It still haunts him.

His dark eyes search mine, and there's a vulnerability to them that he hasn't shown me before. Since

I've met Marcus, apart from being a little grumpy, he comes across as light-hearted, making jokes like he's got no cares in the world. But I don't know anything that's really going on inside.

My hands go to his cheeks, and I run them over his rough beard. He groans and closes his eyes, leaning into my touch.

My heart thunders in my chest. I want to ease his pain. I want to kiss it out of him, to give him some comfort and take his darkness.

When he opens his eyes, there's fire in them. The spark is back.

His hand clasps my wrist, and the pressure makes me gasp.

"Touching me like that isn't going to get you your story." His voice is as raspy and ragged as the emotions on his face.

"I don't care about the story." In this moment it's true. What's happening between us is bigger than a story, bigger than my job, bigger than a bunch of unpaid bills. That stuff doesn't matter when I'm looking into the heart and soul of this man. "I care about you."

He groans as I say it, and conflict flashes across his face. Fear and uncertainty.

He's been hurt.

I'm sure of it. The knowledge only makes me

want him more. To ease his troubles, to show him kindness and love.

"Kiss me," I whisper.

Conflict marches across his face, along with desire and uncertainty. The desire wins as he presses his mouth to mine.

It's a slow kiss. A healing kiss, tender and warm. A kiss we both need so badly, a kiss that proves there's still something good in the world.

He gives into it completely. His hands tangle in my hair, and he pulls me toward him. My hands go around his neck, and we embrace like lovers who've known each other for eternity rather than two days.

I lose myself in the kiss, in the sweet oblivion of his warmth.

The stillness of the workshop is broken by the ringing of my phone vibrating in my back pocket.

For a delicious moment I think of ignoring it, not wanting to break the spell. Then I think of Mom, and I pull away.

"I have to take this," I say when I see Mom's number flash up on the screen.

Marcus looks disappointed, but he doesn't push.

His fingers run down my arm as we pull apart, keeping connected to me until the last minute.

"Is everything okay, Mom?"

I try to keep my voice steady and am relieved to hear Mom sounding cheerful.

"Yes, don't panic. Just wanted to hear your voice."

Guilt gnaws at me. I should be at home with her, not kissing a hot stranger on the mountain. Marcus is watching me, his eyes blazing with promise.

I put the phone on my chest. "I'm going to talk to my mom for a bit."

He nods, understanding. "Of course." He kisses me chastely on the forehead. "I might do some work in here. I'll see you in the morning."

I leave him in the workshop and walk quickly back to my cabin while Mom tells me about her day.

"Only five days till Valentine's Day, Hazel. You got a date yet?"

"Mom." I blush, and even though she can't see me, she catches her breath. Mom is as perceptive as I am.

"You've met a man!" she squeals into the phone and then starts coughing.

"Mom?"

She tries to laugh it off, and I don't let her hear how alarmed I am. I've got one more day here, then I'm back to New York. Back to Mom and the bills and what the hell to do about the story I can't write.

. . .

59

I speak to Mom for half an hour before she gets too tired. Then I pull out my laptop and the notes I've been making about my trip.

Marcus has made it clear he doesn't want to do the feature, but he's too compelling not to write about. No matter where these words end up, I have to get them out of my head and onto the page.

An hour later, I'm stiff from sitting and I'm fighting back tears.

I don't need to know the details of what happened to him over there. His artwork tells enough. I just hope I've done them justice in my description.

I grab a glass of water from the kitchen and notice the light still on in Marcus's workshop. I'm not the only one who likes to work late into the night.

Still not knowing what I'll do with the story, I go back to my laptop and write for another hour.

7
MARCUS

Old sycamores tower above us as I lead Hazel along one of my favorite hiking paths. She keeps her eyes upwards and her mouth open, marveling at every new bird she hears, every ancient tree. It's like she's never been out in nature before. It makes me remember how lucky I am to live out here on the side of the mountain.

I let her go ahead of me, setting the pace and giving me the opportunity to admire her curvy ass.

I've been rock hard for this woman since I saw her in a bath towel. Even before that, since she walked into our clubhouse. And after our kiss last night, I positively *ache* for her.

It's been a long time since I've felt like this about anyone. For many years, I shut myself off. That's what happens when someone betrays you. My thoughts flutter to Karmen, my ex from years ago. It's her betrayal that has kept me a bachelor. But it's been so long since I thought about her that there's not even a trace of heartache.

After kissing Hazel last night, I stayed in my workshop until well past midnight working on a new piece. I felt energized and motivated in a different way than usual.

Usually, it's a nightmare or the memories that get me into the workshop, but this was entirely different. And the piece I'm working on reflects that.

"Where do you get your wood from for your work? Is it from here?" Hazel stops and runs her hand over the bark of a tall pine.

I eye her warily, wondering if she's still trying to get a story out of me. She's naturally curious, and I hope that's all it is because I like talking to her. She's easy to talk to, and I want to share my experiences with her. I want her to know me.

We've been getting to know each other, and my past and my artwork is such a big part of that. I want to tell Hazel my story. Not for some article she's writing, but because I want her to know who I am as a man. And I trust her. When she looks up at me with those round, innocent eyes, how can I not?

"My family runs a sawmill," I tell her. "That's

where I get the wood from. Off cuts that they aren't using."

Her eyebrows come together in the way they do when she's thinking.

"Your family runs the Wild Sawmill. Of course," she mutters to herself. "I've read about the Wild Sawmill. It employs half the people on this side of the mountain. I should have put it together."

She looks generally annoyed with herself, which makes me smile. My angel doesn't like to miss anything.

We keep walking, and I tell her about the family sawmill. How it's been here for generations, and about my brothers who run it.

"Is that what got you into woodcarving? Is it a family tradition?"

I peer at her out of the corner of my eye, trying again to judge if she's pushing for a story. But she looks generally interested.

Interested in me.

The thought makes me warm inside. I'm falling for Hazel, and there's a chance she feels the same. She opened up to me as we were walking and told me about her sick mother. Now, I'm compelled to open up to her.

"I started carving when I came back from the military."

My mind goes back to that time. I came away unscathed, at least physically. But I don't think anyone who goes to war comes back without some damage on the inside. I'm just thankful mine is less serious than most. And I have an outlet.

"It started as a way to do something with my hands."

Our convoy was hit with an IED on my last tour. I was retiring from the military, heading back home to help when my brother took over the sawmill. We were on our way back to base, and I was flying out the next morning. A few of us were leaving and we were joking around, talking about what we'd do when we got back. That's when the IED went off.

I tell Hazel about all of it. About the explosion, then the gunfire. The screams, the blood, the choking smoke, and the stench of burning flesh. The confusion as we opened fire at an unseen enemy.

The horror that leeched into my soul, and the anguish. We sent five men home in body bags from that explosion. But I came away unscathed, not even a scrape, and the guilt haunts me still.

Carving wood, creating something out of nothing, helped keep my hands busy and my mind still. I started out of necessity, and I soon realized I was good at it. It became a hobby, and when Danni opened the studio, she convinced me to exhibit my work and sell a few pieces.

I haven't spoken to anybody about this. Not since my last appointment with the therapist they made me see when I got back. As we talk, the constriction in my chest that I didn't even know I was carrying starts to ease.

Hazel places her hand in mine, and the comfort of having her here beside me makes it easier to keep talking.

I spill it all, telling her about military life and about the artwork. About how I couldn't think straight when I came back and wasn't much use to my brother at the mill. I tell her about the Wild Riders and how the MC saved me. How being on a bike on the mountain was freeing in a way that I needed.

By the time we finish talking, the trail has looped back around to where we left the bike. I lean against it, and Hazel stops in front of me. A ray of pale winter light falls through the trees and falls on her face, making her look even more angelic.

I never knew how good it would feel to talk about everything. But with this woman, I can open my soul to her.

"It's a beautiful story, Marcus," she says. "Just curious, but why don't you want to share it?"

I take both her hands in mine and pull her forward so she's wedged between my thighs. She doesn't resist and I love this feeling between us, this connection that's grown over the last two days.

"Because it's not just my story to tell. People died, Hazel. It's not a story for a fucking arts magazine. People want to find meaning in my woodwork. It's pretty fucking obvious. I'm not going to exploit the lives of those men to sell a few pieces."

She frowns, and I regret my harsh tone.

"I'm sorry if that gets you into trouble," I say more gently. "I told you my story, Hazel, because I want you to know me. But only you. I don't want to put pieces of me out into the world." I take her hands and press them to her chest, right over her heart. "That piece of me is only for you."

It's been such a short time but this woman has stolen my heart, and I hope she feels the same way.

"I understand," she says softly.

She's so beautiful standing here among the trees with the afternoon light making patterns on her skin.

I pull her towards me and our lips meet, like magnets that are drawn together. I kiss her long and hard. She opens her mouth for me and deepens the kiss.

The birds sing around us, soaring on a soft breeze. The chill of the air tickles my skin, and Hazel shivers.

"Come on. Let's get you back to the warm cabin."

I drape my jacket around her as we climb onto my bike. She's a natural on the bike, and I love feeling her arms around me.

It's been the perfect day; I just wish my city girl could stay on the mountain forever.

8

HAZEL

*M*y head is full of the story that Marcus told me on the hike. It reverberates around my brain, threading itself into different passages of time and emotion. I feel for the mountain man, his service to his country, what he experienced in Iraq, and how he's quietly endured the darkness of it ever since. It's an incredible story of hope and sacrifice and the unseen mental health toll war takes on our service men and women.

The ride back on the bike gives me time to silently process all that he's just told me. I'm aching to get my thoughts down in writing, to make sense of what he's told me and weave it into his story.

When we get back to his place, Marcus drops me off at my cabin. Even though I want to spend more time with the big mountain man, I'm relieved when he says he has to stop in at the club. I want to get my thoughts down on paper while they're still fresh in my head.

We agree to meet at his place for dinner. Then he kisses me long and hard until my lips are swollen.

As soon as I'm in the cabin, I make a pot of coffee and pull out my laptop. I still have Marcus's leather jacket with the Wild Riders patch on it, and I pull it around my shoulders as I sit cross-legged on the bed with my laptop on my lap.

My fingers fly over the keys as I get his story down. My heart is breaking all over again as I type it up. But I know Marcus doesn't want my sympathy. He told me his story because he trusts me. Because in the few days that I've been here, there's no denying the connection between us. The impossible connection between a New York girl and a wild mountain man.

I wonder what it would be like to live out here permanently, to not have to go back to a shitty boss and the bustle of the city.

I'm sure it's being around all this nature that has me so inspired as well. I've never written so fast as I do now, with the sounds of the wind blowing in the trees around me and the gentle call of birds. There're no city noises, no city smells, no distractions.

I close my eyes and imagine a life out here in

Marcus's cabin. Growing our own herbs, cooking together, him quietly working in his workshop while I write.

My phone buzzes, and it's Mom. Guilt floods me as my fantasy vanishes. Of course I can't leave Mom alone, even if he was into me for more than a few days' fling. I put the fantasy aside and answer the call.

A few hours later, we're seated at Marcus's table after finishing up dinner. I insisted on cooking tonight, even though mac n' cheese is about the only thing I know how to make. I don't have much time to cook at home, and it's usually beige food from the freezer or a ready meal. I can practically feel myself getting healthier out here.

I'm pushing the last bit of macaroni around my plate, thinking about Mom and wondering what she's having to eat.

She seemed fine when I talked to her. Only four days till V Day, she merrily reminded me. Which is a reminder that I need to get back. My flight leaves tomorrow at midday. And as much as I can't wait to get back to Mom, I'm dreading leaving Marcus. Dreading getting back to my bills and debts and real life. This has been a good distraction, but it's only that.

"What are you thinking about?"

My head snaps up to find Marcus crouched beside my chair, a half amused smile on his face.

"You look like you've got the weight of the world on your shoulders."

His soft brown eyes are full of genuine concern.

"Just thinking about Mom." Which is half the truth. I haven't told him about my debts. It's not something I want to discuss.

"You want to give her a call?"

"I already did. She's fine. It's just... four days till Valentine's Day..."

He doesn't laugh at me. Instead he takes my hand, acknowledging my concern about the family curse.

"You leave tomorrow." His voice is quiet, resigned.

I want him to ask me to stay with him here on the mountain. But he doesn't. He won't. Not now that he knows about my mom.

"Yes. I need to get back to her. It might be..." I can't finish the sentence.

It might be her last few days in this realm. I should be on the plane right now; I shouldn't have even come. But there's a chance that the Valentine's curse is bullshit, and Mom will keep hanging on. I'm holding onto that chance.

"Oh angel, I'm sorry."

Marcus pulls me to my feet and puts his arms

around me. I lean into him, into his solid body, and feel warmth spread through me. He won't ask me to stay. I get that, but maybe for one night I can forget about everything. For one night, I can do something reckless and fun, something for myself before I go back and face my real life.

He kisses me then, a slow, tender kiss that I feel all the way to my bones. My body heats, and along with the comfort comes a slow burning need. My skin prickles, and my body responds to him. My pussy flutters to life, and damp heat spreads between my legs.

The kiss deepens, and his hands run though my hair.

"Can I stay here tonight?" I ask.

He catches his breath and pulls my head back to look in my eyes. They're full of heat, a mirror of my own.

"Is that what you want, angel?"

"Yes."

I want to forget. I want to lose myself in this amazing, thoughtful, troubled man. For one night, I want to forget.

9

MARCUS

I lead Hazel to the bedroom as the anticipation builds in my chest. Ever since I first laid eyes on my angel, I knew she'd be mine. Now it's time to claim her.

I don't know what will happen tomorrow when it's her time to leave. I can't ask her to stay, not when her mother's ill, not when her home is in New York. But I can't be without her.

There have got to be suburbs in New York that have parks and open areas. We could live outside the city and get the best of both worlds. Sure, there are no mountains, but as long as I've got some wilderness, I'll be happy. It'll mean leaving the MC, but maybe I can start a New York branch. There have got to be veterans who need support in the city.

The city will be stifling, but I'll do it for Hazel in a heartbeat.

It's this future I'm thinking of as I lay her down on my bed. I climb on top of her, and our bodies collide as my mouth explores every part of her, kissing her neck, her throat, her chest. I open her shirt and run my hands over her luscious breasts, loving the way she moans at my touch. Her eyelids flutter shut and her lips purse as the most delicious sounds come out of her mouth.

She's responsive to my touch and I enjoy caressing her, exploring her body as I ease her out of her clothes.

When I've got Hazel naked before me, her hair splayed out on the pillow, I sit back and admire her body, tracing the lines of her curves with my fingertips.

"You're beautiful, angel."

She smiles shyly at me, all traces of the confident city girl wiped away in this moment.

She sits up, and her hands fumble with my jeans. She's clumsy and nervous, and I stop her hands and capture her chin.

"Slow down, angel. We've got all night."

"Sorry," she mumbles and bites her lower lip. "It's just . . . I've never done this before."

Does she mean hook up with a virtual stranger?

Because I feel like I've known this woman half my life.

"This isn't a one night stand, Hazel."

Her eyes meet mine, wide and innocent and afraid.

"How can it not be?" she whispers.

I kiss her gently on the lips and pull back. I gave my heart to a woman once before, and she betrayed me. For years I kept myself closed off, but in a matter of days Hazel has torn down every defense I have. She already has my heart and my soul. She doesn't know it yet, but I'll do whatever it takes to be with her.

"Have faith, Hazel. Enjoy tonight, and we'll figure out tomorrow, tomorrow."

Her curious eyes scan mine, and I wonder what's going on in that overworked brain of hers.

I've never seen anyone who needs a release more, and that's exactly what I'm going to give her.

"Lie back."

She hesitates. "I meant I haven't done *it* before."

My heart forgets to beat. "You're a virgin?"

She looks down. "Yes."

This moment just got heavier and more special, but she doesn't see it that way.

"I want to be your first, Hazel, and your last."

I cup her chin, and she looks up at me. "I'll make this good for you. Trust me."

She nods and relaxes, a smile spreading across her face.

I push her gently down on the bed and run my hands over her body. She moans as I touch every sensitive part, making her writhe on the bed.

Dipping between her legs, I lick the sensitive nub of her sex. Her hips buck forward, and I hold her in place as I flutter my tongue over her clit.

Hazel clings onto the bedsheets as I draw out her pleasure, moving fast then slow until she's begging me to let her come. I insert one finger and then two and her pussy clamps around me, so tight and tender and needy.

"Please, Marcus, please."

But I don't let up until she's panting my name and her hands are tangled in my hair as she pulls my face onto her. Only then do I give her the release she needs, made all the stronger by the delay. She screams my name as her body goes rigid. I keep the pressure on and my two fingers inside her.

When she comes down from her high, I'm there and I'm ready. Her eyes go wide when she sees my cock grasped in my fist, hard and glistening with pre-cum.

I pull a condom from the bedside table, but she shakes her head.

"I'm on birth control if you're clean."

It's been a long time since I was with a woman, and now the thought of nothing being between us has my cock jerking.

One day I'll put a baby in her belly, but that's a conversation for another day.

"This might hurt, angel, but cling on and it'll feel good soon."

She tenses but nods, and I trace circles around her entrance until I feel her relax. I should go slow but she's open before me, glistening and inviting. I thrust inside, and she cries out as my dick slams into her.

"Marcus..."

She half sits up, her fingernails clawing into the skin on my shoulder.

"Look at me," I instruct, and her gaze finds mine. "And breathe."

We take two deep breaths together and Hazel starts to relax, her pussy releasing me from its vice-like grip.

Slowly, I edge into her a little more. This time she pants hard as my cock enters her, and the tightness, the rawness of her makes my balls pull up tight. I'm not going to last long in her virgin pussy. She feels too damn good.

We move together, slowly at first and getting faster as she gets used to the sensation. Her legs wrap around my waist and she draws me to her, wiggling her hips to catch her release. I don't hold back, and as she comes I do too, releasing my load with a shout that matches her screams.

We cling together for a long time, panting in unison, our heartbeats syncing.

As I pull out of her, sticky cum mingled with her virgin blood coats my cock and trickles down her thighs. The sight of her virginity on my cock makes me hard again.

But I need to give her a rest. I grab a warm flannel from the bathroom and gently wipe the stickiness from her thighs.

Afterwards, I lie next to Hazel and pull her close. She's where she's supposed to be tonight, in my arms. Tomorrow, we'll figure out the rest.

All I know is this woman is my future. Whatever I have to do, she's mine.

HAZEL

*T*he next morning I stretch lazily, enjoying the dull ache between my legs that reminds me of last night.

We woke in the night to make love again, and then a third time in the predawn light. The last time was intense, clinging to each other, fearing it might be the last.

Marcus said this isn't a one night thing, but I don't see a way that we can be together.

There's no way I can move out here. Not with Mom the way she is, and besides, what would I do for work? I've got bills to pay, and that's the reality of life. I need to be in New York for my job and for Mom.

But I can't ask Marcus to move to the city. I know he would if I ask. But he belongs here in the wilderness with his art and his MC. So I don't say anything as we eat breakfast together, the silence heavy with things unsaid.

I take a shower, and when I come out the cabin is silent. There's a note on the table from Marcus saying he's in his workshop and he'll see me soon for coffee.

I smile at his barely legible scrawl. He's an artist alright, through and through with the messy hand-writing to prove it.

It's a few hours before I have to leave for my flight, but I understand why Marcus has gone to the workshop.

Last night has left me feeling inspired, and I head to my cabin to type up my thoughts.

It's a crisp morning but a little warmer than it's been, and winter sun breaks through the trees.

I leave the door to the cabin open, enjoying the fresh breeze and the sounds of birdsong. My mind feels sharp surrounded by nature, and I perch on the stool by the kitchen counter and open my laptop.

As usual, my mind's spinning with every revelation about Marcus. My fingers fly over the keyboard as I get them out of my head and onto the page.

It's about thirty minutes later when my phone rings.

I stretch as I stand up, and my heart sinks when I

see that it's Scott. I put the phone on speaker and put it down on the counter so I can make a pot of coffee.

"Have you got the story?" There are no formalities. He gets straight to the point. I squeeze my eyes shut and press my temple with my thumb and forefinger.

"Did you get him to talk, Hazel?"

Scott's New York accent sounds hard, impatient, and I can hear the sounds of traffic in the background. He's probably got his phone headset on as he walks from the subway to the office.

"Kinda."

I've been trying not to think about my job. About what it will mean to not turn in the story.

I don't want to tell Scott over the phone. If he fires me, it will ruin my day, and I want one more good day. One last good memory before I'm unemployed with a stack of medical bills.

If I can just get through this phone conversation, I won't have to face him till I get back to the office. And then I'll deal with whatever I have to deal with.

I'll get a job stacking shelves in the local grocery store if I need to. I can write in the evenings, do freelance work, do whatever it takes to pay the bills.

"What do you mean, kinda? Hazel, have you got the story or not?"

I press my lips together as I pour hot coffee into

my mug. I hate lying, but I really don't want to have this conversation now.

"Yeah, I got him to talk."

"That's my girl." Scott sounds happy, which is rare for him. "I knew you had it in you, Hazel. Let me guess. He was a hot-blooded man after all?"

Anger flares in my chest at the way he's talking about Marcus. I want to tell him that he's a human being. He's not just a story. But instead I take a deep breath before I say something I'm going to regret.

"Yeah," I say, my voice on edge. "I guess it worked. I got him to talk."

I pick up my coffee, and I turn around. My heart leaps into my throat. Marcus is standing in the doorway.

I give a startled gasp and drop my coffee. Hot liquid splashes up my legs and I jump back before it scalds me, muttering a string of curses.

"Did you drop something?" Scott calls down the phone. "Don't tell me you got it on your laptop."

I push the hang up button, not wanting Scott to be privy to anything that's about to happen.

"You wrote the story?"

Marcus's face is full of disbelief. He wants me to deny it, and I wish I could.

My eyes dart to the open laptop on the counter, and he follows my gaze. I take a step toward my laptop, but he's too quick and snatches it off the counter.

"It's not what it looks like."

He scans the words, his expression turning hard as he reads.

"I just had to get it out. It's not..."

But his stony expression stops me in my tracks. He places the laptop carefully on the counter. His eyes are full of hurt, and I hate that I've made him feel that way.

"I guess you did everything you could to get the story, huh?"

My heart sinks. That's what I said to Scott, but it's not true.

I shake my head. "No, no, it's not like that."

He holds a hand up to silence me, his expression cold.

"Make sure the heat is off and put the key under the mat when you leave."

My heart clenches at his cold words. I'm just his guest now.

"Marcus..."

He heads down the porch steps and I go to follow him, but my foot comes down on a piece of the broken mug. Sharp pain pierces my foot, and when I look down it's bleeding.

"Damn it."

I find a first aid kit under the sink and stick a bandage over the cut to stop the bleeding. There's the roar of a motorbike, and when I look up Marcus is tearing up the drive, kicking up dust in his haste to get away from me.

Damn. It's an hour until my train from Hope that will take me to the airport.

I want to follow him, but I can't afford to miss the flight. I need to get back to Mom. Besides, he thinks I betrayed him, and I kind of did. I wrote up his story, the story he told for me alone. He doesn't know that I wasn't going to publish it.

It hurts that he didn't stick around to hear my explanation, that he thinks I'd betray him so easily. But maybe it's better this way.

It was stupid to think we could be together. Maybe it's best that we part like this rather than me making him miserable in New York.

The best thing I can do now is go home to Mom.

11

MARCUS

*T*he wind whips at my cheeks as I careen down the mountain. There's a hairpin turn and I lean into it, but I'm going way too fast. Gravel kicks up behind me as I skid and almost lose control. But I don't slow down. My heart is breaking in my chest, and the pain is making me reckless.

I'm not sure where I'm going, just away from her, away from Hazel. I was ready to give her my heart, to move to the city for her, to do whatever it takes to be with her. But it turns out she was just using me to get the story.

In my mind I replay every exchange between us over the last few days, every conversation, every smile, every kiss. I thought it was real, but she was faking it to get her story.

I've been such a dumbass. I knew women were

deceitful. I've been deceived once before, when I came back from my first tour to find my girlfriend had been sleeping with someone else.

I've never been in a relationship since, and that was ten years ago. I keep away from women, knowing how deceitful they can be. But I thought Hazel was different. I trusted her. And I'm a fool for doing so.

I whizz past an overlook and cringe when I see the sheriff's car parked up. I'm going way too fast, and Badge knows it.

It's no surprise when the car pulls out behind me, his lights flashing.

"Shit."

I slow down and pull over next chance I get, which is at a small parking area by a popular walking path.

I'm breathing hard, anger pounding in my veins when Badge strides over.

"What the fuck, Marcus? You must have been doing at least seventy."

He's pissed, and I'm not surprised considering his past. Badge loves to ride as much as the rest of us, but he's a stickler for the speed limit, and the blood alcohol limit. He's been known to hide a man's keys if he's had too much to drink.

He takes his job as Sheriff seriously, to protect

the residents of Wild from harm, and in a remote place like this, that harm is likely to come from the road. He should know that more than anyone.

"Is there an emergency? Do you need a lift?"

"No." I hang my head.

I let my emotions control me, and I was driving recklessly. I wouldn't blame him for giving me a ticket.

"Is your girl in trouble?" It's about the only other excuse there is for speeding on these roads.

"She's not my girl," I hiss through gritted teeth.

Badge takes a step back and eyes me knowingly.

"What happened?" His tone is softer, the friend now, not the Sheriff.

"She never was my girl, Badge."

He gives a soft laugh. "Are you kidding me? I saw the way you two couldn't keep your eyes off each other."

"She's just another manipulative female."

But the words sound wrong to me. Hazel was so different from Karmen, my ex. Karmen was always sly. She was always trying to make me jealous. We were only teenagers when we got together, and she liked to make me prove how much I loved her.

When I look back now, I realize I never really loved her. I loved the idea of her, of being with someone. But it never felt the way it did with Hazel.

87

Badge is frowning at me. "That's harsh, bro. What did she do?"

I explain about the story and the conversation I overheard.

Yeah, I got him to talk.

She got me to talk all right. I bared my soul for my angel. I told her everything I'd kept locked up for years.

I tell Badge about the open laptop that I saw with my own eyes. I thought we were falling in love, but she was using me to get a story.

I don't tell Badge about taking her virginity, although she probably lied about that.

But there was blood.

When I finish talking, Badge is staring at me.

"And what did she say when you asked her about it?"

I squint up at him as a pang of doubt unfurls in my stomach.

"You did let her explain, didn't you?"

I scratch my beard, thinking back over the last twenty minutes. I was so angry about the betrayal that I bolted. I told Hazel where to leave the key, and I got on my bike and got out of there.

"I don't need any more of her lies. She wrote the story, Badge. I saw it on her laptop."

He nods, but he doesn't look convinced. "If that's what she said."

Did she say it? I didn't give her a chance to explain. But I saw it there on the screen. She lied, and she betrayed me.

But there was real blood.

No one would give up their virginity for a story, would they?

I shake the thought out of my head. I was let down once by a woman, and it was stupid of me to trust one again.

"I need a drink."

It's not even midday, but Badge only raises an eyebrow.

"Take it easy. No more speeding, and I'll drive you home if you have too much."

He slaps me on the shoulder before heading back to his car.

I continue down the mountain to the clubhouse. If I turn around now, Hazel will only be full of excuses. I've heard them all before, and I don't want a scene.

Besides, what if I'm right? I can't face going back there to find out that I'm right, that she was lying.

With a heavy heart, I continue down the mountain.

12

HAZEL

Valentine's Day...

*M*om's hand clasps mine as I sit in the armchair next to her bed. An anxious knot has been gnawing at my stomach all day, wondering if this is the last day I'll spend with her. My mood is made all the heavier by the fact that my heart feels like it's cleaved in two.

After the time we spent together, I can't believe Marcus left without letting me explain. But then I don't blame him. I know how that phone call sounded, and he saw the notes I'd typed up. Everything pointed to me seducing him for a story.

My cheeks blaze with anger just thinking about it. I thought we had a connection, but if he thinks I'd sink so low, then he doesn't know me at all.

I'm trying to tell myself it's for the best anyway. I could never take him away from the mountain. It would never have worked. It's best if I remember the good parts about the weekend and try to forget how it ended.

There's a firm pressure on my fingers, and when I look up Mom's frowning at me.

"Are you still thinking about that boy?"

It's funny to hear the burly Marcus being described as a boy. I told Mom all about my time in the mountain. We always share everything, and it took her mind off her own worries for a while.

"If it was meant to be, it will be."

Her voice is firm, as if this is the be all and end all advice on relationships. I try to muster up a smile. It was easy for my parents; they were so much in love there was never any doubt.

"I guess it wasn't meant to be then."

Mom shakes her head. "It's not over yet, hon. Remember what day it is today. Magical things happen for our family on Valentine's Day."

She's got a sparkle in her eye and her smile is mischievous, not masking any pain at all.

I move to sit on the bed next to her, and she shuffles over to make room for me. I peer at her, trying to read the lines of her face.

"How are you feeling, Mom?"

I've been so caught up in my own heartache that I haven't really being paying attention to Mom. To how much firmer her grip is, the laughter in her eyes, her steady, strong voice.

"I feel a lot better, honey. Over the last week, it's like I'm getting my strength back."

That's when it hits me. Mom isn't going to die today. Not this week, not this month.

I grab the chart at the bottom of her bed and flick through the bloodwork. She's been a patient long enough that I can interpret the numbers and the doctor's scrawly handwriting.

Instead of the decline I've been expecting, Mom's blood work is improving.

"Are you in remission?" It comes out as a whisper because I'm too scared to ask.

"No." She shakes her head, but there's no sadness, only acceptance.

"There's no remission for me, Hazel, but I am feeling better. I may not beat this cancer, but I'm sure as hell not going to let it take me just yet."

My mouth drops open. Mom's been accepting of her passing and ready to see Dad again. It's what's been keeping her spirits up this past year.

"But... how about Dad? And meeting him in the next realm?"

She shrugs. "I've got a feeling there's something I

need to do in this realm first."

Her eyes move behind me, and I spin around to see the receptionist coming through the curtains.

"There's someone here to see you. But he's not on the visitor list."

Mom gives a knowing smile, and for a wild moment I wonder if she's met a man online. But it's me the receptionist directs her gaze at.

"A Marcus Wild."

My heart does a double flip in my chest. "Marcus...is here?"

My gaze darts to my mother, and she nods sagely like she was expecting this. How do mothers do that? They know things before they happen.

"Go." She nudges me off the bed. "Go see your valentine."

"He's not my valentine," I mutter as I run a hand through my hair. I'm regretting not washing it last night, but personal appearance has not been at the top of my agenda since I got back.

I rummage in my bag for some lip gloss. It will have to do. It buys me some time as I try to get my thumping heart under control.

Marcus towers over the reception desk, looking like a giant in the small space. His gaze rests on mine, and his expression is unreadable.

My smile dies on my lips. He hasn't come for me; he's come for the story.

I emailed him a copy of what I wrote up with a note that I wasn't going to publish it. But I wanted him to have it. He's come to start a fight with me again for what he thinks I did, for using my feminine wiles to get him talking.

"Walk with me."

The sound of his gravelly voice has my knees quivering, and my core gives a persistent tug. Damn this man for having such an effect on my body.

He opens the door for me, and I step out into the small garden that's part of the care facility. Snowdrops scatter the garden beds and line the small path that leads around the side of the building. The cold air makes me shiver, and I wrap my arms around myself.

"The story's good," he says. "Why aren't you publishing it?"

His expression is still unreadable, cold. But I must be missing something.

"Because you asked me not to. I don't publish without the subject's permission; I would never do that."

I'm insulted that he would even ask. I'm an ethical journalist. Not all journalists are, but I am.

"It's a story that needs to be told. You've done an amazing job."

The praise from Marcus is worth more than any from my boss. It's his story, and for him to think that I captured it right means the world to me.

"I quit my job."

His expression softens for the first time, and he takes a step toward me. His presence this close sets my pulse skipping. I look into his eyes, and there's hurt and hope fighting for space in his heart.

"I know. I went looking for you. Some asshole tried to get me thrown out of the building."

My mouth drops open. "Scott?"

He nods. "That's the guy. Didn't take kindly to me ruffling his shirt up."

"What did you do to him?" The image of Scott facing off with Marcus makes me think of a Chihuahua yapping at a Great Dane.

"He tried to tell me you were a crap writer. So I grabbed him by the lapels."

I giggle, and some of the tension goes out of the air. It's what I've wanted to do to my boss, my ex-boss, a million times.

"Why did you go looking for me?"

I scan his face looking for the truth, hoping like hell it was because of me and not the story.

"Because I didn't give you a chance to explain.

Because I jumped to conclusions. Because the two days I spent with you were the happiest of my life and the two days without you the most miserable.

"I never told you everything that happened with my ex. I came back from tour and found her in bed with my best friend. It was Valentine's Day."

I almost laugh at the irony; how can a day of love be so cursed? But it explains a lot.

"So you jumped to conclusions about me."

He looks pained to admit it.

"I'm sorry I did. But I was wrong. I trust you, Hazel, because I trust what we had was real. At least, I hope it was. I had to come here to make sure, or I'd kick myself for the rest of my life."

My breath hitches. I reach my hand out for him and press it against his cheek.

"I wrote the story up because that's how I process the world. I write. I was never going to give it to Scott without your permission. What we had was real, Marcus. I felt every part of it with you. I had to come back to be with my mother, but I left a part of me on that mountain. A part of my heart with you."

He catches my hand and presses it to his mouth. His lips move over my skin, and the heat skitters up my veins and into my heart.

"I'm such a dumbass. Can you forgive me?"

There are tears in the corners of my eyes,

because there's nothing to forgive. I understand why he reacted like he did, and it's a relief to know that he doesn't doubt me now.

"There's nothing to forgive."

He pulls me toward him and presses his lips to mine. I sink into the kiss, giving myself over to him.

"I'll move here, Hazel. I can sell the cabin and find a place with a workshop..."

I shake my head, because I could never ask that of him. "I don't want you to leave the mountain. I have to be here with my mom, but after..." I can't say the words. Because how can I grieve for someone but also make plans for when they're gone?

"Shhh." His hands clasp mine. "Your mom is the most important thing right now. We'll do what we need to do for her and then figure out our future together. We don't need all the answers now. In fact, there's only one answer I need right now."

He slides down on one knee, his pants getting wet on the snow-covered ground.

"Hazel Lumley, will you marry me?"

Shock makes my mouth drop open. But there's another feeling. As I look into the eyes of this kind, patient man who's been through hell and heartache, I feel a deep connection, a soul connection. I know with certainty that this was meant to be. Up until this point our souls have been adrift, and they've finally found each other.

"Yes," I squeal.

I've known this man only a short time, but it feels like forever. My mom is right. Maybe our souls have always been together, and we've finally found each other in this realm.

Whatever it is, Marcus is the man for me, and whatever the future holds, we'll face it together.

EPILOGUE

HAZEL

Two years later...

"*T*his is the place."

My feet sink into the springy moss covered ground as I step into the ring of ancient oaks.

This was my mother's favorite place in the woods. She would sit here for hours, claiming the ancient oaks had healing powers. I'm not sure if it's true, but they gave her comfort in the last months of her life.

We moved Mom into the small cabin where I first stayed with Marcus and got a part-time nurse for her. It was wonderful having Mom close by as Marcus and I settled into our life together.

After reading the story I wrote about him, Marcus insisted I publish it, but not for an arts magazine. He saw how it could help people understand what some veterans go through and how it might help others in pain. I submitted it to *Time* magazine, and it was published a few months later.

I've been working as a freelance journalist ever since. The stories take me away for a few days here and there, but I love coming back to the mountain and writing it all up in the peacefulness of the cabin.

When I finally told Marcus about my debts, he insisted on paying them off. I earn good money from my writing now, and together we were able to make Mom comfortable and get her the care she needed.

Marcus slides the baby backpack off and gets Maria out of the harness. She was born on February 15th, breaking the Valentine's Day curse.

I no longer get anxious every time February 14th rolls around. Now it's a day to celebrate and to love, and that's why it was Mom's wishes to sprinkle her ashes today, on Valentine's Day. She said the three happiest moments of her life happened on this day: meeting dad, getting married, and having me.

I pull the heavy urn out of my backpack, and we stand together in the center of the ancient oak circle. I hold the urn in the air and a breeze picks up, whistling through the trees and rustling the leaves.

I say the words that Mom wanted, a pagan prayer to guide her to the next realm.

She wanted no tears today, and so I imagine her and Dad meeting up again, wherever they are. I imagine how happy they'll be to see each other as their souls entwine.

I think about all the love in my life, the past two years with Marcus, and how happy Mom was when she walked me down the aisle on our wedding day. How she held Maria in her arms and learned the news a few weeks ago of the new baby growing in my belly.

I scatter the ashes in a circle like she wanted, allowing some to fall into the stream to be carried down the mountain.

It's a quiet ceremony and we walk back hand in hand, not talking, just letting the sounds of the mountain permeate our thoughts.

Mom has passed on, but I still have a lot to be grateful for.

Maria fusses in the baby backpack, so I take her out and carry her on my hip the rest of the way home.

She makes gurgling noises at me, trying to form

her first sounds. Her wide eyes take in everything in the woods, and she giggles at the birds we see.

I sing to her as we walk, and Marcus puts his arm around me. In a few months, we'll welcome her baby brother into our family.

We're starting our new traditions, our new special days as we grow our family.

* * *

BONUS SCENE

How hectic is family life on the mountain for Hazel and Marcus when they've got four kids, and can they all fit in Danni's Caddy?

Read the Wild Valentine bonus scene when you sign up to the Sadie King mailing list.

To get the bonus scene visit:
authorsadieking.com/bonus-scenes

Already a subscriber? Check your last email for the link to access all the bonus content.

This ex-military biker will do anything to protect the people of Wild Heart Mountain, but this runaway bride will test him in ways that will either heal him or break him in two...

I find her walking barefoot on the mountain road, the runaway bride with nowhere to go.

Grace is everything I've forgotten how to be: fun, spontaneous, happy . . .and reckless.

But when she goes too far, how can I protect her?

I've already lost someone to the mountain. I can't risk losing another...

Wild Promises is a runaway bride, age gap romance featuring an OTT ex-military man in uniform and the curvy younger woman who runs away with his heart.

WILD PROMISES

CHAPTER ONE

Calvin

The gravelly strains of Johnny Cash crackle through the car speakers, singing about sorrow and redemption as I tap along on the steering wheel. The late morning sun spills through the autumn-tainted trees, bathing the road in gold dappled light.

I've been patrolling these roads for the last six years, ever since I came back from the armed forces and settled on the side of Wild Heart Mountain, but the beauty of a sunny fall morning gets me every time.

Maybe it's the red maple trees that line this section of the road, or the cliff edge that drops dramatically to the forest below, or the harsh crags of rock that jut out in jaunty angles amongst the greenery, but the scenery here never ceases to take my breath away and calm my soul. And as sheriff of Wild, I need all the calm I can get.

I helped my buddy Symon, who's the Mountain Ranger, check hunting licenses this morning, starting early at the camping sites up on the ridge.

It's the same groups who come back every year, and most have the correct paperwork and respect the animals and the environment, but there are always a few who try to hunt without a license.

There was one this morning, a young guy who didn't have a license and was getting aggressive. When I checked his truck for good measure, I found a bag of pot in the glove box. That's the kind of idiot I don't need on my mountain. I don't care about the tourists who have a puff around the campfire. Unless they're being rowdy, I ignore the sweet scent of weed when I do night patrols. But getting high and handling a firearm? Not on my mountain.

I took him in and booked him, which he wasn't happy about. Kept going on about his rights, but it's the rights of everyone else on the mountain I care about.

There's a serpentine curve in the road, and I slow

down for the corners. Travelling these roads day in and day out means I could drive with my eyes closed and never miss a turn, not that I would.

I've handed out three speeding tickets today already and run breathalyzers on five people before they set off from the campground. All tested within the limit, but the message is clear. I don't tolerate drinking or speeding on my mountain.

The locals know it, but the tourists are another matter.

After the hairpin turn, there's a straight stretch. I hate this part of the road. Drivers speed up, assuming the twists and turns are behind them, then get caught at the next corner. I've had to pull more than one car out of the bushes along the shoulder. Thankfully, no one has ever gone right over.

I slow down in anticipation, never knowing what I'm going to find around the corner.

However, it's not a car this time but a woman on the side of the road.

She's walking on the side of the cliff drop with her back to the oncoming cars and her thumb sticking out. She doesn't even look behind her when she hears my car, just sticks her thumb out further into the road.

Her white dress billows out behind her, caught in

the wind, the fabric so floaty it might pick her up and take her right off the mountain like a parachute. Her dark hair is half pulled up in an elaborate style, with half of it hanging loose in thick curls down her back. Something dangles in her other hand, and as I get closer I make out a pair of high heels, her fingers looped around the back of them. She's barefoot.

"What the fuck..."

Of all the dangerous things this woman's doing-- hitchhiking for a start, walking away from oncoming traffic, not turning when she hears a car-- it's the bare feet that make my lips press together in anger.

I pull onto the shoulder in front of her where there's barely enough room to get my SUV off the road. My seatbelt's unclipped before the car has stopped moving, and I yank the door open.

"What the hell are you..."

She stops walking to stare at me, and the words die on my lips. She's beautiful. Like, autumn morning on the mountain beautiful. With full berry-red lips and a round face, her dark green eyes are bolded with makeup and regard me curiously.

The wind changes suddenly and the billowing dress presses against her body, outlining her full figure: thick thighs, wide hips, and two pillowy breasts, perfect orbs that take up her entire chest and then some.

My mouth goes dry, and I lick my lips. It's an effort to tear my gaze away from her luscious breasts, but somehow I manage it. I look down and get a glimpse of her bare feet. The toenails are painted bright pink, and they're covered in road dust and grazes.

"You can't walk around here in bare feet."

My tone comes out harsh, and she looks down at her feet.

"Is that a crime, sheriff?"

Her voice is sweet and playful, and when I dare to look up, she's smiling at me. The breath goes out of my lungs, and I have to look away. Damn, she's gorgeous, but this isn't a laughing matter.

"We've got snakes around here, and there could be glass on the road. You might hurt your...ah...feet."

This woman has got me tongue-tied like a teenager.

She arches an eyebrow at me, and the smile turns to a smirk. "I'm thankful for your concern for my feet."

Damn, this isn't about her feet. I want to shake her for all the stupid things she's doing.

"You shouldn't hitch around here. It's dangerous."

"But it's not illegal."

Her emerald green eyes sparkle with a challenge. I'm trying to keep her safe, and she thinks this is a game.

"Get in the car."

The smirk slides off her face, and it feels satisfying.

"But I haven't done anything wrong."

I open the door to the back seat for her and she stands there, not moving.

"You're not under arrest," I reassure her. "I'm giving you your next ride."

She smiles again, that same smile as if she's laughing at me. "You haven't even asked where I'm going."

"I don't care where you're going. Just get in the car and I'll take you wherever you want to go. But you're not hitching in bare feet on my goddam mountain."

Her brow furrows, and she stares at me defiantly.

"I haven't done anything wrong, sheriff."

"Haven't done anything wrong?" I run a hand through my hair, my exasperation building with every minute we stand here. "You should walk on the side of the road facing oncoming traffic so you don't get hit. You should wear shoes outside, and most importantly you shouldn't be hitching in the first place. Any stranger could pick you up. I'd rather give you a lift now than have to deal with a homicide investigation when they find your body on the side of the road."

She looks startled, and I instantly regret my last words. I run my hand through my hair.

"Will you just get in the goddamn car? Please?"

She folds her arms and looks at me with a frown creasing her brow.

"But *you're* a stranger."

I hold her gaze, unsure if she's teasing me or if she's always this exasperating.

"I'm the sheriff." I sweep my arm toward the patrol car with *Sheriff* written on the side and red and blue lights on top. Then I pull out my badge and hold it out to her.

She regards the car and leans forward to study my badge. The scent of sweet feminine perfume accosts my nostrils, and I breathe in deeply. Goddamn, she smells as good as she looks, and that scent is waking up parts of my body that have been dormant for months. I step back before the twinge in my loins can turn into anything else.

The woman looks up from my badge.

"How do I know it's not fake?"

I press my lips together and snap my badge closed. My gaze snaps to the valley, and I search for the calm the view usually brings out in me. It's not cool to get angry with civilians, but this woman is pushing me to the limit.

When I turn back, she's grinning.

"I'm just fucking with you, sheriff." She slaps me on the shoulder. "I'd love a lift. Thanks."

She slides into the back seat chuckling to herself. Her eyes sparkle, causing adorable creases to form at the edges. Yup, she's laughing at me.

I'm frozen in place. I've never encountered anyone who makes me so exasperated, yet I want to slide into the backseat next to her, to smell her perfume again, to make her laugh with me and not at me. To show her that I'm not always an uptight asshole. Only when someone is doing something stupid like hitching in bare feet.

As she goes to pull the door closed behind her, one of the shoes drops to the ground. She reaches for it, but I crouch down and get it first.

The shoe is a white satin heel with a tiny cluster of pearls on one side.

There's only one reason a woman wears white satin heels. My gaze goes to the dress that falls elegantly around her legs.

It's satin too, a simple V-neck design, but there's a string of tiny pearls sewn into the neckline.

"Is that... a wedding dress?"

The woman bites her lip and her gaze shifts to the window, her voice barely audible.

"It's a long story."

"Ah shit," I mutter.

She's not just hitching in bare feet. This woman's a runaway bride.

To keep reading visit:
mybook.to/WRMCWildPromises

All the Scars we Cannot See

What the Fudge

Fudge and the Firefighter

The Seal's Obsession

His Big Book Stack

For a full list of Sadie King's books check out her website

www.authorsadieking.com

ABOUT THE AUTHOR

Sadie King is a USA Today Best Selling Author of contemporary romance novellas.

She lives in New Zealand with her ex-military husband and raucous young son.

When she's not writing she loves catching waves with her son, running along the beach, and drinking good wine with a book in hand.

Keep in touch when you sign up for her newsletter. You'll snag yourself a free short romance and access to all the bonus content!

authorsadieking.com/bonus-scenes

Printed in Great Britain
by Amazon

52093515R00072